MOONE BOY
THE MARVELLOUS ACTIVITY MANUAL

THIS BOOK BELONGS TO

....

Also available

Moone Boy: The Blunder Years
Moone Boy: The Fish Detective

CHRIS O'DOWD
& NICK V. MURPHY

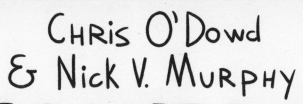

MOONE BOY
THE MARVELLOUS ACTIVITY MANUAL

ILLUSTRATED BY
WALTER GIAMPAGLIA
OF CARTOON SALOON

MACMILLAN
CHILDREN'S BOOKS

First published 2016 by Macmillan Children's Books
an imprint of Pan Macmillan
20 New Wharf Road, London N1 9RR
Associated companies throughout the world
www.panmacmillan.com

ISBN 978-1-5098-3259-0

1 3 5 7 9 8 6 4 2

A CIP catalogue record for this book is available from
the British Library.

Printed and bound by CPI Group (UK) Ltd, Croydon CR0 4YY

I'd like to dedicate this book to my brother John, a wild and funny soul with superb Uncle-ing skills. He only managed to escape inclusion in the Moone Boy family due to him being incredibly old.

Chris

For all the Beavers, Rainbows, Cubs, Brownies, Scouts, Girl Guides, and especially my own Scouting big brothers who inspired some of these stories – Killian who got ejected from the boat, and Luke who rejected the jacks.

Nick

INTRODUCTION

Greetings, fellow Earthling!

Or, for those reading the Martian edition –

⚫◻♏♦✕■♓• ♠✳︎☺◻♦✕☺✎ ♥■ ♏☺♦ ○♏

Welcome to *The Marvellous Activity Manual*.

My name is Sean 'Caution' Murphy, seventh son of Norman 'Nervous' Murphy and Carmel 'Careful' Murphy. Yes, both of their surnames were Murphy, as they were also very distant cousins.

1

You may know me better as the handsome, dynamic and deeply humble imaginary friend of Martin Moone of Boyle, Ireland. I shall be your chapter chaperone through the pages of this barmy book, this jovial journal, this little ledger of 'LOLs'.

Firstly, congratulations on your purchase of this copy of *Moone Boy: The Marvellous Activity Manual*. As you may have noticed, this is no ordinary book. This is an *activity* book. Most books just sit there and tell you one long story, like a jabbering old man who smells like soggy shoes. But not this book, no sir! This is a book that runs around the room like its pants are on fire, while juggling pineapples and playing the kazoo.

'But what does it do?' I hear you ask.

What *doesn't* it do, more like?!

Dance. Sadly, we couldn't get it to dance, due to a dispute with the union of Irish Book Jivers. But it does pretty much everything else. We've got short stories, a comic strip, games, puzzles, jokes and crafts for those with nimble fingers. We even provide snacks (if you enjoy the taste of stale paper).

In *Moone Boy: The Blunder Years*, Martin Moone had a tricky time finding a suitable IF. Imaginary friends like me don't grow on trees. We are grown *under* trees. Kinda. But it's a tricky process and we'd like to help.

In this book, I shall guide you down the prickly path of discovering your own imaginary friend. And an imaginary friend can be quite the discovery, like an untouched tropical golden island or a dirty penny down the back of an armchair. Think of your imagination as the last unconquered land, and your mind a great oak boat with soaring sails and rats fleeing from the hull.

As discovering a suitable IF can be a gruelling task, I strongly suggest you take your time. An entire year in fact. It may well be a good idea to quit school, move into your attic and focus entirely on nothing but this book for the next

3

twelve months (or seven 'yections', which you'll know about if you've read *Moone Boy: The Fish Detective*).

OK, it's time to hit the high seas! If you need a wee, now would be a good moment: there are no loos aboard the good ship 'book'.

So turn on the attic light, untie your reality ropes, and let's cast off from Boredom Bay. It's time to set sail with me, Captain Sean Murphy, and First Mate Martin Moone on this *Marvellous Activity Manual* adventure!

Ahoy!

Caution

YECTIONS

A year is a very long time when you're an idiot. To cope with the curse of the calendar, Martin Moone has developed the habit of dividing the year into smaller sections, or 'yections'. As you complete each yection, you'll be one step closer to creating your perfect IF!

ACTIVITY

KEEP OUT!

OK, we've got a lot to do and you're going to need to focus. We want no interruptions. So try hanging one of these on your bedroom door.

Use the picture opposite as a guide to make your own hanger – you could make it bigger, or even stick it on to cardboard to make it stronger. Colour it in or add the scariest face you can think of to keep intruders at bay.

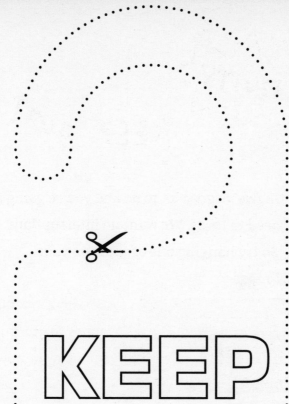

KEEP
OUT
IF-making
in progress

YECTION 1

BOXING FOR LOVE

It's the post-Christmas lull. The last of the choccies have disappeared (except for the creams), your new woolly jumper is starting to smell, and so is your grandad, who refuses to go home. But then at last, Yection 1 finally arrives with New Year's Day!

The New Year is a time of great change and possibility – anything can happen! It's a time for making lists, and changing jumpers, and tricking Grandad into going outside and then locking the door behind him.

9

It's a time to start fresh. A clean slate. A new era. A new you. And what better way to do that than by getting yourself a brand new IF! Right?

Well hold on just one second. Calm the flip down. Unlike puppies, imaginary friends aren't just for Christmas. They're for life! Or until you get bored of them and just stop imagining them. But either way, it's a big decision and needs some thought.

So, before we jump in, it's time to ask yourself some important questions . . .

iMAGiNARY FRiEND

By Authority of the Corporate League of Imaginary Friends Federation

To Whom It May Concern

On this day....SATURDAY THE 6TH OF NOVEMBER......in the place of..JUST OUTSIDE...
BOYLE.in the county of ...ROSCOMMON...in the country of ..IRELAND.
on the planet of ..THE..EARTH......,
we hereby certify that this person, animal, beast, blob or other
weird creature, will henceforth go by the name of SEAN "CAUTION" MURPHY
and is hereby licensed to practise as an ..IMAGINARY FRIEND.in accordance with
the Laws, Codes and Ideals of Imaginary Friendship as set out in *The Big
Massive Manual*, somewhere near the middle.

Hurrah!

Signed by: *Meng the Magpie*

Witnessed by: *Bruce the Spruce*

Second witness: CRUNCHiE HAYSTACKS

C.L.I.F.F.

11

ACTIVITY DO YOU NEED AN IMAGINARY FRIEND?

Do you have brothers or sisters who steal your stuff or draw on your face?

Do you need help with your homework but don't want to ask an actual person?

Have you always wanted a wingman, wingwoman, or wing-alien?

YES

NO

Follow this flowchart to see if you really need an IF. You can start with any of the questions.

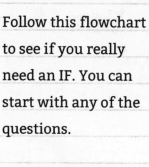

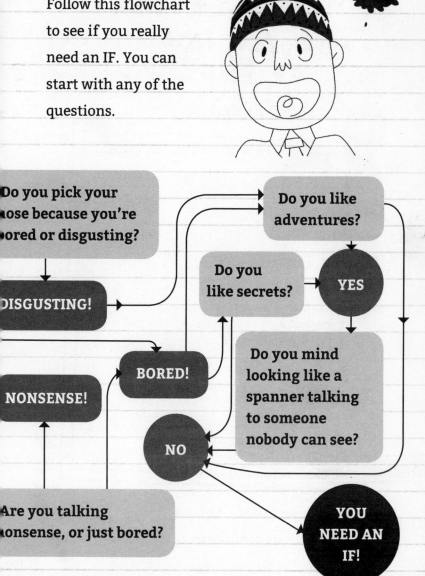

Do you pick your nose because you're bored or disgusting?

Do you like adventures?

Do you like secrets?

DISGUSTING!

YES

Do you mind looking like a spanner talking to someone nobody can see?

BORED!

NONSENSE!

NO

Are you talking nonsense, or just bored?

YOU NEED AN IF!

IS THERE ROOM IN YOUR HOUSE FOR AN IMAGINARY FRIEND?

This is Martin's family.

FIDELMA

TRISHA

DAD AND MAM

SINEAD

MARTIN

As you can see, the Moone home is pretty jammers. But even this six-foot-tall imaginary wingman is pretty good at fitting into small spaces.

This is because my first job involved a lot of time spent travelling between wardrobes – one of the main portals into the imaginary world ... Draw your own family below and see if there's any room left in the house for your new IF.

The good news is that imaginary friends are very space-efficient. We come in all shapes and sizes to suit your needs. If you've got plenty of room in your house, then you could get an enormous IF and let it bound around to its heart's content. But if you're tighter on space, then you could get one so small that they can fit inside your pencil case.

IF RESIDENCE – INSERT PENCILS AT YOUR PERIL!

They can sleep in a drawer, your shoe, or
even on your ceiling if they've got suction
hands, like my friend Ollie 'Octo' O'Reilly.
Personally, I like to curl up at the foot of
Martin's bed like a loyal Labrador. But as soon as
he's asleep, I high-tail it back to the Imaginary
Friends' Break Room for a cup of rumble juice
and a nice foot massage from Keith, an ogre
with the hands of an angel!

WHAT THE FLIP SHOULD I CALL MY IF?

One of the most important steps in creating an imaginary friend is choosing their name. Every IF has three names – like Sean 'Caution' Murphy, or Crunchie 'Danger' Haystacks.

FELICITY 'FANTABULOUS' FRUMP

PILE-DRIVER 'POOKIE' PET

TENNESSEE 'TOOTIN'' TOM

LOOPY 'LOOPINGTON' LO

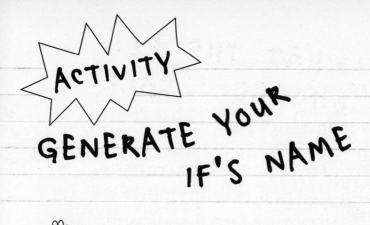

ACTIVITY

GENERATE YOUR IF'S NAME

 Find out your IF's name with this name builder.

1. Find the second letter of your own first name.

A-ANTSY
B-BOUNCY
C-CLUMSY
D-DITZY
E-ELECTRIFYING
F-FUZZY
G-GRUBBY
H-HAIRY
I-ITCHY
J-JAZZY
K-KOOKY
L-LUMPY
M-MIGHTY

N-NUTTY
O-OCTOHANDS
P-PRICKLY
Q-QUIET
R-ROWDY
S-SPOTTED
T-TRICKY
U-UPPITY
V-VIVACIOUS
W-WITTY
X-X-CELLENT
Y-YAPPY
Z-ZESTY

write the word in here ➔

2. Find the last letter of your first name.

A-ANTEATER
B-BRAINIAC
C-THE CAPTAIN
D-DESTRUCTO
E-THE ERASER
F-FUSSYPANTS
G-GRANDMASTER
H-HUGSALOT
I-THE ICICLE
J-JIGGLESON
K-KICKMEISTER
L-LUNCHBOX
M-MCPANCAKE

N-NECKTIE
O-O'DAZZLE
P-PRISSYFITZ
Q-QUACKERS
R-RATTLESNAKE
S-SMELLINGTON
T-TYRANNOSAURUS
U-UMBRELLAHEAD
V-VON STINKENSTEIN
W-WARNING
X-THE X-TERMINATOR
Y-YOGAPANTS
Z-THE ZOOKEEPER

write the word in here

3. Find the last letter of your surname.

A-ADDISON
B-BAILEY
C-CASEY
D-DYLAN
E-EMERY
F-FAYE
G-GLEN
H-HUNTER
I-IGUANA

J-JAMIE
K-KENDALL
L-LANE
M-MORGAN
N-NOEL
O-ORION
P-PARKER
Q-QUINN
R-RILEY

S-SIDNEY
T-TORY
U-URI
V-VAN
W-WINNIE
X-XAVIER
Y-YUMI
Z-ZANE

write the
word in here

4. Put all three words together and you have your IF's name. Now fill it in and draw a picture of him or her below.

MEET MY IMAGINARY FRIEND:

← draw them in here

ACTIVITY

BE MY IF

It's Valentine's Day, and with romance in the air, you need to ask yourself – *am I looking for an imaginary girlfriend or imaginary boyfriend?* If you are, then that is a terrible idea! Imaginary friends are the worst boyfriends and girlfriends ever. We're invisible, so it's really hard to hug us, and we're always broke, so we never buy you any presents. But we still like getting Valentine's cards! Who doesn't like that? So if you're feeling creative, try making a Valentine's card for your new IF.

1. Find a piece of card which can be the base for your IF's card (maybe your IF's favourite colour) and fold it in half.

2. Get some red card and cut out a huge love heart to stick on the card.

3. Add any other decoration or text you want on to the card – the bigger the better. Stickers, drawings, poems . . .

WILL YOU BE MY IF CRISP THIS VALENTINE'S?

♡ ♡ ♡ ♡

DID I MENTION I LOVE CRISPS?

23

4. Tell your IF you're glad
you've found them with
a soppy message.

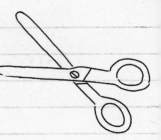

5. Keep the element of surprise by
asking another IF to deliver it for you. But
be careful – they love tricking realsies, and
might accidentally deliver your card to
Crunchie Haystacks instead . . .

MARCH MADNESS

'Bahahahahahahaha!'

Martin shook with laughter until the milk from his Readybix cereal started to trickle out of his nose.

READYBIX
- CEREAL -
New Extra Day Recipe!
BE LIKE THE READYBIX KID!
COLLECT 50 TOKENS
AND GET A FREE
READYBIX BIKE!

1 kg.

His sister, Sinead, was less amused. 'What's so funny, Snot Milk?'

'*You?*' he spluttered, 'In ... the *Girl Guides?*'

'So?' she snapped.

So? *So?* Allow me to explain. Sinead was the most evil of Martin's fearsome threesome of sisters. And that's saying something – she had a lot of competition from Trisha and Fidelma. But

25

Sinead was the sort of girl who'd abandon her own hamster in a forest just so that Martin wouldn't be able to cuddle it. So when she announced that she was joining the Girl Guides, it was like the Wicked Witch of the West joining the Care Bears.

'Can I tie some knots?' Martin sniggered in a girly voice.

'Bob a job, sir, bob a job*!' I chuckled, in a manly voice.

Martin howled, getting dangerously close to wetting himself.

'Giggle away, ya spanner,' said Sinead snarkily. 'I'll be the one laughing when I'm marching in the Saint Patrick's Day parade!'

*BOB A JOB — odd jobs to raise money for the Scouts. 'Bob' is another word for 'cash', as money was invented by a man called Bob Spondulix, along with his nephew, Bob Syour Uncle.

MOONE DICTIONARY

Our chuckles came to an abrupt halt.

'Huh?' asked Martin.

'You heard me, muck-for-brains. The Girl Guides march every year! I'll be marching with the army and the firemen and even that fella in the Dracula costume on the cement factory's truck.'

Martin looked gobsmacked. 'You'll be in the parade? With Count Concrete?'

'I'm gonna *rule* the parade, Dork Dip. I've joined the Girl Guides so I can win first prize this year. That trophy for "Best Marchers, Decorated Lorry, or Leprechaun Beard" will be mine – ours, I mean!'

She gave a triumphant cackle and skipped away, leaving Martin looking rather perturbed, with a face full of envy and a nose full of milk.

'This is so unfair!' moaned Martin, as we trudged to school.

'It's an outrage!' I agreed.

'There's only one Moone who should be

marching in that parade, and it's not her.'

'Absolutely, it should be your dad. He loves walking.'

'Not Dad – *me!* I'm way better at walking than any of them!' he bragged. 'Do you think I should join the firemen?'

'Well, as your trusty imaginary friend, I'd have to advise against that, Martin, since they've already turned you down four times this year. And don't forget, you *are* allergic to fire.'

'Curse my delicate skin,' muttered Martin.

'But hey,' I suggested, trying to perk him up, 'maybe there's some sort of . . . Man Guides that you can join.'

His face lit up excitedly. *'Man Guides?!'*

'Man Guides?' echoed an equally excited voice behind us.

It was Martin's best (non-imaginary) friend, Padraic, who was also on his way to school.

'Hey P-Bomb!'

'Whattup, Moonbeam?'

28

They did a complicated handshake that concluded with a couple of knee slaps and then continued on their way together.

'So, what's all this talk about Man Guides?' asked Padraic.

'Does such a thing exist?' asked Martin.

'Of course it exists! I'm one of them! And we go by many names.'

'Like what?'

'"Scouts" . . . Well, just "Scouts" really. But it's so great, Martin! We camp. We tie knots. We march in the parade. We wear uniforms with woggles—'

'Enough!' interrupted Martin. 'You had me at 'camp'. And also at 'woggles'. I don't know what they are, but I want one. Can you get me in, Padraic?'

Padraic paused, and looked Martin up and down. 'Hmmm. I'm not sure you're really Scouts material, Martin.'

'C'mon, P-diddly. I was *born* to be a Scout! I've always wanted to be a Scout! Ever since

I heard about them just now!'

'Well, I can't make any promises. But I'll do my best,' Padraic assured him. 'It's really up to Bagheera,' he added, and strolled on.

Martin and I looked at each other. 'Bagheera*?'

That night, Padraic marched Martin up to the Scouts Hall and banged on the door with a complicated secret knock.

Rat-ta-tat-ta-bomp-tat! Thumpitty-thump-rat-tat-tat-thump!

No one answered.

So then he rang the secret door bell.

Ding-ding-dong-doopity-dong-doopity-ding!

No one answered.

So then he just opened the door and we went inside.

We found 'Bagheera' in the hall, playing a rowdy game of Hacky Sack with the Scouts. It

*BAGHEERA — a black panther, who's kind of the 'Irish mammy' of *The Jungle Book*, telling Mowgli to stop acting the monkey and sending him home for his tea.

MOONE DICTIONARY

turned out that
Bagheera was
actually Gerry
Bonner, father of
the infamous
Bonner brothers.
He was wearing
a green Scouts jumper that was way
too small for him and could barely
contain his bulging belly as he leapt around
after the tiny bean bag. The soundtrack to *The
Jungle Book* movie was blaring from a cassette
player.

'Patrol Leader Baloo reporting for duty!'
called Padraic towards the happy Hacky
Sackers. But they didn't seem to hear him.

'*Baloo?*' asked Martin, confused.

'We all have names from *The Jungle Book*,'
explained Padraic proudly.

Martin looked at him blankly.

Padraic shrugged. 'It's a Scouts thing.'

He turned back to the others and yelled over

the music. 'Bagheera sir! I bring a new recruit!'

This time, Gerry Bonner turned his sweaty face towards them and snapped off the music. The room fell silent and all eyes turned to Martin.

'A new recruit?' asked Gerry. 'And who might that be?'

Martin spoke up nervously. 'Me, sir. Martin Moone. I want to be a man guide.'

Gerry smiled, amused. 'Hear that, gang? A man cub who wants to be a man guide.'

The boys all laughed.

I chuckled too. 'They seem like a happy bunch,' I whispered to Martin.

Gerry approached Martin slowly. For a portly man he had a rather dainty walk, and reeked of aftershave and cream buns. 'We don't *guide*, Martin Moone. We scout! And we don't just let anyone join, no sir.' Gerry leaned closer. 'Answer me this. Have you ever camped in the wilds?'

Martin thought about this. 'I fell asleep in the shed once,' he offered.

'Can you handle a knife?'

'I'm the fastest butterer in Boyle.'

'Ever roasted a pig?'

'No, but I once kept a mouse in my pocket for a whole afternoon and he got pretty toasty.'

Gerry didn't seem impressed. 'Hmm. One last question, Martin. Do you have ten pence for membership?'

'Probably.'

'OK, you're in!'

'Yes!' cried Martin, punching the air with joy. He asked if he could be called 'Mowgli', but that name had already been taken by Other Alan, a boy from Martin's class whose surname had always been a mystery because Martin never bothered to remember it. Gerry explained that there weren't enough characters from *The Jungle Book* movie to go around, so everyone else was named after other Disney characters.

'So who will I be?' asked Martin.

'You'll be . . .' said Gerry, regarding the boy thoughtfully, 'Dumbo.'

'*Dumbo?!*'

'It's not ideal,' I agreed. 'But who cares, buddy? We're in! We're gonna be in the parade!'

Martin smiled happily and we shared a small, secret high-five.

The countdown to Saint Patrick's Day had begun and Martin had a lot to learn. So he learned hard and he learned fast.

Then he forgot most of it. So he learned it again. Harder and faster.

But he forgot it again. So then he learned it really slowly and carefully. And that time it stuck.

He learned how to tie a scout's neckerchief, how to identify a shamrock, and even how to knit a leprechaun's beard.

How to knit a leprechaun's beard

In 104 easy steps

Martin's middle sister, Trisha, regarded Saint Patrick's Day as the dumbest day of the year. To a goth girl who always wore black, green outfits made her physically ill, especially when folks adorned them with clumps of weeds and lined the streets to applaud a tractor with a balloon on it.

'It's a sham!' she ranted. 'Snakes? Shamrocks? Leprechauns? How could anyone believe in that sack of nonsense! The Moones should have nothing to do with it!'

But when she saw Martin attempting to knit his beard, she shoved him aside, unable to watch him make such a mess of it. 'Idiot! You're doing it wrong!' she barked, and took over the task herself. Martin's uselessness had always reaped rewards.

Martin loved his new Scouts uniform, particularly his woggle, which looked like a shiny conker with a hole in the middle of it, much like a competition conker. He also just liked saying the word 'woggle'. But we weren't there to just stand around saying the word 'woggle'. We were there to march. And by flip did we march!

Well – Martin marched. I mostly just sat in a tree and watched them traipse around in the muck while Gerry Bonner roared at them.

'Baloo, you're out of step! Dumbo, lift your knees! Cinderella, you're going the wrong way! You've got to listen to the beat, lads! The beat of your feet! It's music!' implored Gerry, waltzing with himself alongside the marching Scouts. 'To march is to dance! And to dance is to march!'

Gerry had some strange teaching techniques. He even taught the boys how to do an Irish jig so that they'd lift their knees properly. Then sometimes he'd yell at them 'Companyyyyy MARCH!' and other times he'd yell 'Companyyyy JIG!' just to keep them on their toes.

*

36

Meanwhile, Sinead was rising through the ranks of the Girl Guides, attempting to transform the girl group from a collection of delightful do-gooders into her own private army who stomped around Boyle like a squadron of Stormtroopers. Martin did his best to ignore them, trying to master his own march-skills. So when Saint Patrick's Day arrived, he was finally ready.

There was much excitement as the marchers lined up behind the floats and decorated lorries. Even Francie Feeley had a float-a-boat-shaped truck with a few hairy 'mermaids' from the fish factory laying around him, smoking cigarettes. He had buckets of fish ready to throw to the crowd, which were starting to stink in the sun.

'Let's get this show on the road!'

yelled Francie to the dapper Dracula on the cement factory truck.

'Any sec now, Francie!' called Count Concrete, who was trying to wipe the sweat off his pointy collar.

It was a weirdly sunny day and I told Martin that he was starting to turn pink.

'Curse my delicate skin,' grumbled the boy.

Padraic was slathering himself up with suncream and tossed the bottle to Martin with a wink. *'Always be prepared!'*

'Oh, we're prepared all right,' came a familiar voice behind them. It was Sinead with her renegade group of Girl gangsters lined up, ready to march.

Sinead leaned closer to her brother and said, menacingly, 'If you Scout saps think you're gonna win that trophy, you've got another thing coming.'

'What sort of "thing"?' asked Martin curiously.

Sinead just gave an evil grin. Something

glistened at her feet, and then Martin saw that they were wearing steel-capped boots.

'Woah!' I whispered, shocked. 'Are those even legal?!'

But before he could answer, Gerry gave his familiar call of 'Companyyyyy MARCH!' and we were off.

Soon the Scouts were marching through town while Sinead and her fearsome followers stomped right behind them, in perfect time. Martin and Padraic were at the back of the platoon, and were getting kicked in the keister* with every step!

'Yowch!' wailed Padraic, as they marched. 'I can't take much more of this!'

'Me neither, my buns are turning blue!' moaned Martin. 'What are we going to do?'

Luckily, Martin had his trusty imaginary

*KEISTER — word #184 for bum.

MOONE DICTIONARY

friend who was never short of ideas, and when I told him my plan, Martin put on his deepest voice and yelled out, 'Companyyyyy JIG!'

Like trained dogs, the Scouts immediately launched into a lively jig. Prancing around on the road, Martin and Padraic could now easily avoid the arse assault, and the crowd seemed to enjoy it too, cheering for the flouncing fellas.

'Why are ye dancing?' hissed Gerry at his Scouts.

'I thought to dance *was* to march,' replied a confused Trevor.

'Shut up, Pocahontas. Companyyyyy MARCH!' yelled Gerry.

And the Scouts went back to their march.

Thump Thump! went Sinead's steel toes into Martin's tuckus*.

'Companyyyyy JIG!' he yelled. And the Scouts broke ranks again, hopping and twirling like they were in a barn dance.

'Companyyyyy MARCH!'

'Companyyyyy JIG!'

'MARCH!'

'JIG!'

'MARCH!'

'JIG!'

'MARCH! MARCH! MARCH!'

'JIG! JIG! JIG!'

Completely confused, the half-marching-half-jigging Scouts were now approaching the bandstand where the Mayor and the

*TUCKUS — word #209 for bum. This one comes from the Yiddish word 'tuches' as in, 'nobody tuches my tuckus'.

MOONE DICTIONARY

41

Bishop and all the important people in Boyle were surveying the celebrations, judging the marchers.

Desperate to see them fail, Sinead tried to give Martin one last boot, but he dodge-jigged it nicely and she kicked Padraic's suncream out of his pocket instead. The girls stomped over the bottle, squirting it everywhere, and suddenly all of them went flying on the slippery surface. They tumbled over each other in a chaotic heap of skirts, pigtails, and steel-toed boots.

Martin and Padraic whooped with delight and jigged triumphantly past the bandstand with the Scouts. The Mayor seemed impressed with their new marching moves, and when the parade was over, he stood up to the mic.

'I believe we have a winner!' announced the Mayor.

He picked up the huge, shiny trophy. 'Winner of the Best Marchers, Decorated Lorry, or Leprechaun Beard is . . .'

Martin adjusted his woggle in readiness.

'. . . That young lady over there!'

Martin froze.

The Mayor was pointing at a skinny goth girl who was sporting a lush leprechaun's beard.

I squinted. 'Wait a second. Is that . . . ?'

'*Trisha?!*' gasped Martin and Sinead at the same time.

Trisha strolled past them both, grinning broadly beneath her bushy beard, and hopped onstage to claim her trophy.

Martin was dumbstruck. 'But . . . you don't even believe in Saint Patrick's Day!'

Trisha gave a shrug. 'I believe in beating you two losers!'

Martin sighed, defeated. He and Sinead both looked at each other glumly.

'Beaten by a beard,' murmured Sinead. 'It's even worse than being beaten by *you*.'

Martin nodded in agreement. 'It actually is.'

The pair watched gloomily as Trisha posed for photographs with the mayor.

'Want to wait till she's asleep and grab

that trophy?' asked Sinead.

'We could bring it to Padraic's farm and tie it to their manure spreader?' suggested Martin.

Sinead smiled. 'I know some excellent knots now.'

Martin looked at her. 'Me too, sis. Me too.'

The pair shook hands, regarding each other with respect for the first time. It was like there was a new understanding between them – the dawning of a new era of cooperation and reconciliation.

'You know what, Sinead?' said Martin. 'If we just worked together instead of trying to destroy each other, there's really nothing we couldn't accomplish.'

Sinead nodded slowly. 'Well let's not go mad, Martin.'

'Agreed,' said Martin. 'I'm not sure what came over me there.'

'See ya around, woggle head,' she said, and sauntered off.

Martin turned back to me and winced with

the pain in his rear end from Sinead's booting. 'C'mon Sean, let's head home, and grab a big tub of ice cream.'

'Sounds like a plan, buddy!'

'And sit my bare bruised buttocks right on top of it.'

That wasn't quite my idea of a fun Friday night, so I swiftly backtracked. 'Eh. Actually . . . I think I hear someone calling me in the imaginary world,' I lied, pretending to hear imaginary voices. 'What's that, Loopy Lou? Right now? I'm on my way!' I yelled.

And with that,

Poof!

I was gone.

YECTION 2

LOVEFOOL

Now you've got an IF with a nifty name, it's time to give them some equally nifty headwear. February and March are particularly chilly months, so they'll definitely need a hat. All the best IFs wear hats. And the best of the best wear bobble hats! Untangle the strings opposite to match the hats to their IFs.

Answers on page 194

ACTIVITY

HATS AHOY!

ACTIVITY

TRISHA'S CRAFT CORNER

'Don't be an idiot – no stylish IF is going to want any of those hats. I'm an AMAZING designer! You should use one of my hats instead. Like these ones, which you can just colour in with your own amazing designs.'

ACTIVITY

SEAN'S CRAFT CORNER

Woah, what just happened?! Martin and I left the room for two minutes to make a banana sandwich, and Trisha's scrawled all over the page! And they're useless hats too. Totally flat! If you make a pompom, you can stick that on any hat you like, and look just like me and Martin. Here's how . . .

1. Use a mug to draw two circles on a piece of thick cardboard, and an egg cup to draw two smaller circles inside. Cut out the middle of the circle so you have a cardboard doughnut and put them together. Mmm, doughnuts!

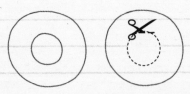

2. Get a ball of wool and cut a *very* long piece

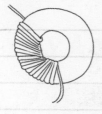

(you can use different colours if you like. My faves are red, black and white, of course). Wind it round and round the cardboard, pushing it through the middle of the circles, until you can't fit any more in. Remember to tie a knot in the end of the wool once your circle is full.

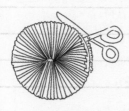

3. Use nail scissors to snip through the wool around the outside edge of the circles.

4. When you've snipped all the way around, pull the cardboard circles apart a bit and tie a length of wool round the middle of the ball. Tie and knot tightly.

5. Carefully remove the two cardboard circles and fluff up your pompom.

It should now look like this. Attach to your favourite hat, *et voila!*

APRIL FOOL'S DAY

This is one of the best days of the year. The only person who loves it more than me is Loopy Lou.

RIGHTY ROO, SEANIE POO! THERE'S NOTHING I LOVE BETTER THAN A PRANKEROO! HERE'S A FEW THAT YOU AND YOUR IF CAN PLAY ON YOUR FRIENDS OR FAMILY AND MAKE THEM LOOK LIKE A BUNCH OF DUM-DUMS.

DRAW LITTLE RED DOTTY DOTS ON THE CENTRE OF THE BATHROOM MIRROR, SO WHEN SOMEONE LOOKS AT THEIR REFLECTION, THEY'LL THINK THEY'RE COVERED IN PIMPLY PIMPLES!

BEFORE YOUR FAVOURITE TV SHOW STARTS, COVER THE FRONT SENSOR OF THE REMOTE CONTROL WITH A PIECE OF STICKY TAPE. WHEN SOMEONE ELSE TRIES TO CHANGE THE CHANNEL — WHOOPSIE! — IT WON'T WORK, AND YOU CAN WATCH YOUR SHOW FOREVER!

TAKE A BATHROOM SPONGE AND COVER IT IN YUMMY CHOCOLATE ICING, SO IT LOOKS LIKE A CAKE. THEN LEAVE IT ON THE KITCHEN COUNTER AND WAIT FOR A HUNGRY VICTIM TO POUNCE!

SISTERS LOVE THEIR BEAUTY SLEEP. BUT YOU CAN PUT A STOP TO THAT BY HIDING LOTS OF ALARM CLOCKS IN THEIR BEDROOM! SET THEM ALL TO GO OFF AT DIFFERENT TIMES IN THE NIGHT AND LIE BACK TO ENJOY THEIR SLEEP-DEPRIVED RAGE!

56

PUT ROCKS IN THE BOTTOM OF YOUR FRIEND'S SCHOOLBAG. GRADUALLY ADD MORE AND MORE ROCKS EACH DAY.

WHY AM I GETTING SO WEAK? MAYBE I SHOULDN'T HAVE EATEN ALL THOSE CHOCOLATE SPONGES.

SUPER-IFS

Having an imaginary friend is like having your own personal superhero! At least, it might be if you get an IF with superpowers. Thankfully, this never occurred to Martin. But you don't seem quite as dopey as him, so maybe you should consider it. However, just remember that Super-IFs tend to rush off a lot to fix their hair or fight imaginary villains. Not like us normal IFs! We have literally nowhere else to be than by your side. And non-super hair requires far less care.

So, instead of fighting crime, we're far more likely to help our Realsies fight boredom! I do this by showing Martin cool stuff like the best way to sharpen a pencil – two turns clockwise, one turn counter-clockwise, three turns clockwise – and how to write HILLBILLIES on his calculator (53177187714).

But on a particularly rainy March day, we might just kick back and make a little comic strip like the one coming up – starring us! We didn't have time to add colour, so why don't you grab your colouring pencils and colour us in as you read? Go on, ya lazy eejit! I should be a nice healthy pink with a bountiful brown beard, and Martin should be a sickly yellow colour with green warts on his face and stink lines coming from his bum.

THE
AMAZING
ADVENTURES
OF
IF MAN
AND
MOONE BOY!

Don't forget to
colour us in!

27 SECONDS LATER...

64

66

67

68

69

70

ACTIVITY

STAR AS A SUPERHERO

'PHEW! THAT WAS EXCITING. IF SEAN AND MARTIN CAN HAVE THEIR OWN COMIC STRIP, SO CAN YOU AND YOUR IF. START OFF YOUR OWN COMIC STRIP WITH YOUR OWN SUPERHERO NAMES. TO GET YOU STARTED, YOU COULD TRY TO COPY MOLE BOY AND GERBIL GENT IN THEIR SUPERHERO OUTFITS . . .'

73

YECTION 3
FOOL'S GOLD

April is the time for Easter! Usually. Easter moves around a lot. I think it depends on when chocolate eggs are ready to be harvested. But if the eggs are taking too long to ripen on their chocolate vines, then why not make yourself a chocolate fish instead? In *The Blunder Years*, Martin never got to taste his chocolate fish because it escaped down the toilet. But if you follow this recipe, then you can make yourself a marvellous melt-in-your-mouth mackerel that's fit for Francie Feeley himself!

SWEET FREEDOM!

ACTIVITY

MAKE A CHOCOLATE FISH

1. Make a batch of cookie dough using your favourite recipe (or buy it in a tub from the supermarket).

2. Roll it out flat until it is about 3mm thick and cut into the shape of a fish (one big one or lots of small ones, using a knife or a cookie cutter).

3. Place the dough shapes on a baking tray and cook according to instructions. Get an adult to help you with the oven. Remove from the oven and leave to cool.

4. Melt some chocolate in the microwave on a low setting, being careful not to burn it.

5. Cover the cooled cookies in the chocolate and place on a baking tray to set.

6. If you want to add scales, decorate your fish with hundreds and thousands or icing.

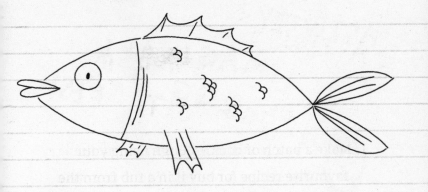

If it doesn't work out quite as well as you'd hoped, then just do what Martin and I do every time we fail at cooking – help yourself to a big bowl of Readybix instead (or any other breakfast cereal that's 90 per cent dust).

READYBIX
- CEREAL -
NEW EXTRA DRY RECIPE!
BE LIKE THE READYBIX KID!
COLLECT 50 TOKENS
AND GET A FREE
READYBIX BIKE!

1 kg.

ACTIVITY

IMAGINARY EGG TREE

If you're still in an Easter mood, then try decorating a real egg Moone Boy style.

1. Nab a freshly-laid egg from under a hen's bum. Or take it out of an egg box – whichever is handier.

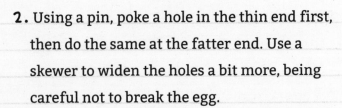

2. Using a pin, poke a hole in the thin end first, then do the same at the fatter end. Use a skewer to widen the holes a bit more, being careful not to break the egg.

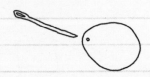

3. Carefully poke a skewer all the way through the egg, from one hole to the other, to break the yolk – do this a few times.

4. Next – over a bowl – blow through the top hole to force out the yolk and all the other eggy gloop. It'll take a few tries, but if you're having trouble, widen the holes a bit more. After lots of huffing and puffing, you should end up with a perfect, empty egg shell!

blow in here

5. Now for the creative part! Grab your paints or colouring pencils and decorate your own Moone Boy-style egg! You could make an eggy Martin, Crunchie, Padraic, or Yours Truly!

6. Next, take a piece of thread and tie it to half a matchstick – the wooden bit, not the fire-making bit! Poke the matchstick through the top hole so it jams inside the egg, keep the thread outside and tie in a loop. Now you've got an egg on a string.

7. Grab a branch or twig that looks like Bruce the Spruce. Stick it in a vase, hang your eggs from it, and hey presto, you've just made your very own Moone Boy Imaginary Egg Tree!

ACTIVITY

FIND A CATCHPHRASE!

Now that you're on a sugar high from your chocolate fish and feeling a bit dizzy from blowing the gloop out of that egg, it's the perfect time to think about your new IF's catchphrase! A catchphrase says a lot about your IF. Take Martin's first imaginary friend, Loopy Lou, for example. His catchphrases are:

OH NO HE DIDN'T!

I GOTS TO GET ME ONE OF THOSE!

WHOOPSIE!

From these you know right away:

1. He has quite a lot of accidents.
2. He's a flippin' idiot.

My own catchphrase is 'Aw balls'. However, this wasn't supposed to be my catchphrase. I wanted my catchphrase to be 'This is the single greatest day of my life!' But I don't get to say that very often. Or ever. 'Aw balls' has become my catchphrase because Martin messes up a lot. This catchphrase tells you:

> 1. I'VE GOT A USELESS REALSIE.

> 2. HE'S A FLIPPIN' IDIOT.

Turn the page to find a catchprase for your IF.

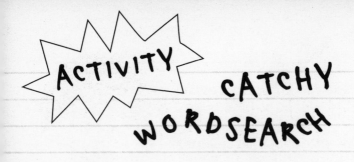

Either come up with your own catchphrase for your new IF, or find one in this Catchy Wordsearch. I've done the first one for you . . .

YOU'RE A POST	GAS FELLA
FIDDLESTICKS	WHAT'S THE CRAIC?
WHISHT!	YUP
HAPPY AS LARRY	IT'S ON
AMADAN	OH NO, HE DIDN'T!
GENIE MAC	SLAP MY BELLY!
RADICAL!	~~AW BALLS!~~
SOUND!	WHOOPSIE!

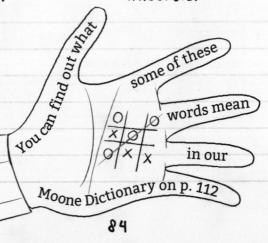

You can find out what some of these words mean in our Moone Dictionary on p. 112

A	T	Y	S	A	J	K	F	M	L	A	R	H	S
G	Y	O	U	R	E	A	P	O	S	T	N	F	L
M	P	F	B	F	L	W	T	H	O	H	B	G	A
L	C	D	I	R	N	B	G	A	U	I	W	C	P
T	A	H	S	D	S	A	J	E	N	F	H	H	M
I	I	L	W	Y	D	L	Q	S	D	W	A	E	Y
H	I	X	O	R	R	L	Y	G	A	S	T	Y	B
F	J	T	P	K	J	S	E	A	G	T	S	N	E
W	H	I	S	H	T	Z	D	S	H	L	T	E	L
S	A	W	J	O	L	S	S	F	T	W	H	Y	L
W	P	O	A	S	N	I	L	E	W	I	E	J	Y
M	P	Q	H	T	S	M	U	L	R	D	C	L	Q
R	Y	R	G	N	R	H	C	L	Y	G	R	K	R
K	A	L	E	I	O	P	Y	A	U	J	A	T	S
P	S	D	N	Q	W	H	O	O	P	S	I	E	M
I	L	P	I	R	H	Y	E	G	K	B	C	W	L
W	A	F	E	C	U	Q	J	D	Z	P	I	F	S
K	R	S	M	L	A	V	E	L	I	J	P	O	D
Z	R	M	A	D	E	L	C	F	S	D	L	H	F
C	Y	N	C	G	K	A	M	A	D	A	N	K	A
X	I	Y	K	J	D	G	H	D	G	K	D	T	J

85

Answers on page 194

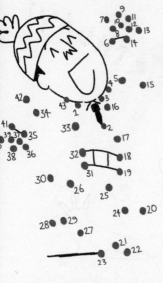

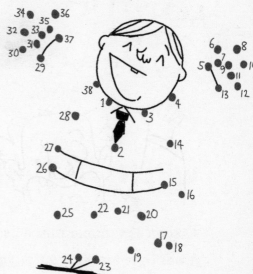

Martin has
thrown me
an imaginary
party. Join the
dots to complete
the guestlist,
and colour
us in when
you've finished!

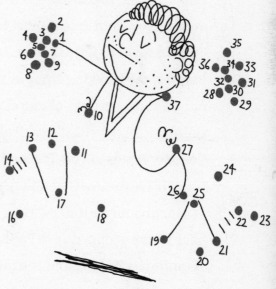

WHEN NATURE CALLS

As soon as summer raised its big shiny head,
it was time for the scout troop to go camping.
On a brisk June morning, twenty fearless
fellas packed their woggles in their backpacks
and bravely ventured almost two whole miles
outside town to Boyle Forest. Led by Gerry
Bonner, the trekking troop whistled various
out-of-tune versions of cub classics: 'We're
Going on a Bear Hunt' and 'Take Me Home,
Country Roads'. Even 'Ice Ice Baby' got whistled,
though Trevor insisted on rapping along to it.

Martin and Padraic were propping up the
back of the group, due to Padraic's inconsistent
skipping technique and the fact that Martin

seemed to be carrying quite a severe limp.

'What's up, Martin? Do you have tennis ankle again?'

Martin had recently developed a chronic condition he called 'tennis ankle', which had been caused by his sister Sinead repeatedly thwacking him with a tennis racquet whenever he touched her chips.

'No P, I just really need to go to the toilet.'

'Ah, that explains the shifty shuffle. Why don't you just pee in the bushes?'

Martin seemed a little embarrassed by this suggestion.

'Well, to be honest P-dog, I've never been great at going to the toilet away from our house.'

'That's weird, I'm the complete opposite,' Padraic said. 'I hate using the loo at home.'

'Really, how come?'

'Well, remember when we had that massive storm the winter before last? Dad insisted on moving our chickens into the house to protect them. After they caused chaos in the kitchen, Mam stuck them in the bath. Sixteen of them. It was pretty uncomfortable to feel them all watching me when I did my wee-wees.'

'Right. Wait, what did you do if you needed a bath?'

There was a long pause as Padraic remembered this. His face went from distant recollection, to mild amusement, to utter disgust. He turned back to Martin, forcing an awkward fake smile.

'Let's talk about something else now.'

*

'Home sweet home!' Gerry called as he stopped in a secluded clearing by the lake. A thin smile was lodged on his big sunburnt face as he dropped his giant rucksack to the ground.

'Ye've probably all heard the saying *The journey is better than the destination.* Isn't that what they say, gang?'

The troop shrugged. There were murmurs of 'haven't heard that, no', 'who's *they*?' and, 'I don't know any sayings.'

'Well clearly *they* have never been to Boyle Forest!' Gerry continued. 'What a silly saying! Welcome to your new abode: The Great Outdoors!'

With that, Gerry let out a primal roar and thumped his chest with his fists.

Martin and Padraic looked at each other. Martin had just one question.

'Cool, so where's the hotel?'

'Hotel, schmotel!' Gerry barked back. 'We're in the wild now, boyos. So pitch those tents and get settled in for the night.'

'We're sleeping outside? Have we done something wrong?' I asked.

'This is madness!' Martin agreed.

'What did you think camping was, Moone?'

'I suppose I thought it was some kind of spa treatment,' Martin admitted.

Gerry glared back at him. We had clearly been misinformed.

'So I probably packed badly then?'

We turned to find Crunchie Haystacks dressed in a fluffy white robe and slippers, wearing a green, creamy face-mask.

'Not to worry,' he said, wiping off the gunk and casting aside his robe. 'I'll just go as nature intended!' And he skipped away in his birthday suit.

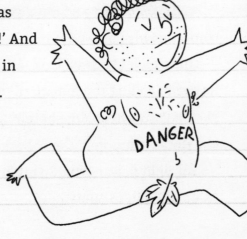

As day turned to night, Martin and

Padraic really struggled to pitch their tent. The ground was too hard, the poles were too soft, the tent fabric was too tight and, of course, the two boys were too stupid. Luckily, they had me and Crunchie to help them find a simple solution.

'It may just be easier to lay the tent fabric out on the ground, lie down on top of it, and roll around until you're both entirely covered.'

'That *would* be snug,' Crunchie agreed.

'So . . . we'd be like . . . human sausage rolls?' asked Martin, unsure.

'*Waterproof* sausage rolls, buddy.'

'And what would we do with the tent poles?'

'Cocktail sticks!' Crunchie replied, with utter confidence.

This answer seemed to please Padraic, and he began rolling the tent out like pastry. But as Martin watched on, he got that flutter from his bladder again.

'All right P, I'm going to investigate the campsite toilet situation.'

'Okey dokey, Martin!' Padraic replied, as he began to roll himself up like an outdoor appetizer.

Martin and I followed our noses to find the troop toilet. The 'facilities' were disappointing, to say the least. As we stood peering down at bright blue liquid bulging from a big black bucket, Martin looked concerned.

'And what, may I ask, am I supposed to do with that nonsense?'

'Just pee in it, buddy,' I said.

'I can't do that, Sean. There must be twenty poos in there!'

'Already? We just got here.'

Just then, Gerry Bonner passed by, looking freshly relieved, as if a great weight had just been lifted off him. Or *out* of him.

Martin winced. 'Peeing outside? I don't know Sean. It's just not natural. I'm not a flippin' Spaniard.'

'Do you mean Spaniel?'

'Yes I do.'

'We're in the wilds now, Martin. We've got to become at one with nature!'

'I'm not doing my number ones in nature,' he insisted.

'So what's your plan, buddy? We're pretty far from civilization here.'

Martin looked puzzled. But as his thinking jelly began to congeal, he walked off with purpose, and with a worsening limp.

We returned to our campsite to find Padraic's head protruding from their tent like a squashed tortoise.

'I've made a decision! I'll just hold it in,' Martin announced.

'For the whole weekend?!'

'Don't worry. If I don't drink anything or accidentally swallow any rain water, I should be fine.'

'That's so brave of you, Martin.'

'Yes, it *is* brave, isn't it? All I need to do is not allow my silly little brain to think of anything but very dry things: sand, toast, windows, my Mam's cooking. Nothing that reminds me that the world has wet things in it.'

'Well that sounds easy enough,' Padraic agreed. 'Anyway, can you help me out of this tent roll? I'm just gonna have a quick mug of tea and hit the lake before it rains.'

'Stop saying wet things!' Martin spluttered.

As the night progressed, the scout trip was going surprisingly well. After their initial settling-in problems, Martin and Padraic really embraced their new roles as 'men of the wild.' They even learned how to cook beans outside.

'All right gang, who here can tell me how to start a fire?' Gerry asked the gathered troop.

All twenty hands shot up.

'Without using petrol.'

Half the hands went down.

'Or a lighter.'

One by one, the rest of the arms dropped, except one.

'Or your mam,' Gerry added.

Martin slowly lowered his hand.

It turns out that if you rub two sticks together for ages and ages, then get frustrated, curse nature, throw the sticks away and just use matches, fires are really easy to start. Gerry also taught the troop a game called 'Is this a knot or is it not?' This pretty straightforward test of knot-tying skills quickly turned into a fiasco when snot was added to the rope. 'Is this snot on the knot?' proved to be wildly popular but deeply divisive.

Martin and Padraic were having a blast, and apart from some particularly hairy ghost stories, Martin rarely came close to wetting himself. The boys went to their rolled up bed as happy as pigs in a blanket*.

*PIGS IN A BLANKET — sausages wrapped in pastry. Far tastier than the similarly named appetisers, 'Ducks in a Dressing Gown,' or 'Mice in a Sack'.

MOONE DICTIONARY

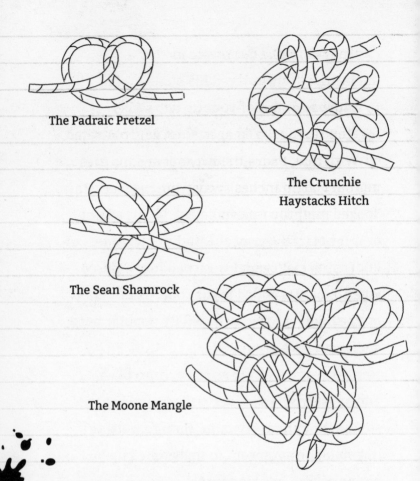

The Padraic Pretzel

The Crunchie
Haystacks Hitch

The Sean Shamrock

The Moone Mangle

Martin woke up the next morning to the strange
sound of Padraic making very loud chicken
noises in his sleep. It sounded insane.

'Ba-ba-ba-ba-back off! Bac-bac-bac-back
offff, chickens!'

'Padraic, wake up. You're having a nightmare!'

'Bac-bac-back offff, ya stupid birds!'

'You're safe, Padraic, there are no birds here.'

With that, Padraic slowly opened his eyes to find Martin inches away from his face. He looked mightily relieved.

'Hey Martin. Sorry about all that.'

'I think maybe you were having a bad dream, P.'

'Yes. I was in the bath at home. And . . . well, anyway . . . Best not discuss it. I think I'll go and splash some water on my face to wake up properly.'

The thought of lovely water made Martin cramp up in agony.

'Aarrgghh, me bladder.'

'Sorry Martin, totally forgot about your tinkle troubles.'

Padraic unrolled himself and skipped off towards the nearest stream, leaving Martin writhing in discomfort.

'Ah, ya poor thing, buddy,' I said sympathetically. 'Remember what we talked about – try and imagine your ribs are like nice long sponges, absorbing all your pee.'

To my surprise, his face suddenly brightened.

'I have a brilliant idea, Sean!'

'Another one?! I can't believe that's possible.'

'I'm going to eat some toilet paper.'

I took a beat to consider this.

'It certainly sounds like a brilliant idea Martin, but I may need you to explain your reasons.'

'Well, once it gets into my belly, it will absorb all my wees.'

'I can't believe I questioned you, Martin. That *is* an excellent idea, if medically unsound!'

Martin hopped up gingerly, just as Gerry Bonner cartwheeled past.

'Excuse me, Mister Bonner?'

'Master Moone, what can I do you for?'

'Well, I was about to use the toilet,' Martin lied.

'Good for you, Moone! But that's not information I want, to be honest.'

'No, I was just wondering where I'd find the toilet paper?'

'Toilet paper, schmoilet paper!' Gerry replied. 'This is a camp, not a holiday camp!'

'But . . . aren't we on holiday?'

'Holidays schmolidays!' Gerry replied, as he cartwheeled off.

For the rest of the morning, Martin tried to keep dry through whatever means necessary. He stared at a tree for a while. He ate the wrapper off someone's ice cream. He sucked on the foam from his sleeping bag.

It was working, somehow. All he had to do now was avoid seeing any flowing water or gushing taps or anything that might trigger the urge to pee.

'Woohoo!' Padraic yelped as he returned from a conker tournament.

'What's going on, P?'

'Gerry's taking us boating on the lake!'

'Aw balls,' I said.

An hour later, we were on a flat-bottomed boat in the middle of Boyle Lake. Gerry had dressed up like a gondolier* and was punting along like a Venetian vicar.

'There's just one rule to punting on a lake. Never drop the pole!' explained Gerry. 'Otherwise we'll be dead in the water! All right, who doesn't want a go with the paddle?'

All hands shot up, terrified of putting their lives in danger. However, Martin was holding his belly in pain, and was the only one without a paw to the sky.

*GONDOLIER — a boatman who rides around on a 'gondola', usually singing operatic songs about ice cream.

MOONE DICTIONARY

'Ah, Moone! I knew you were the adventurous type!'

Martin Moone is many things. A chip thief, a joke forgetter, an amateur fortune-teller. One thing he is not, is a lake boat punter. Within moments of him taking over the punting duties, the long paddle had gotten caught in the thick, mucky lake bed.

'Pull it out!!!' the boys shouted as they watched him struggle.

'Don't drop that pole, Dumbo!' yelled Gerry.

Martin tried desperately to pull it out, but much like his indoor peeing obsession, the paddle was too hard to budge. As the vessel moved onwards, Martin kept his hands gripped on the pole and his feet planted in the boat.

'I'm holding it, I'm holding it!' Martin squeaked.

Seeing his predicament, Padraic grabbed hold of his friend's ankles, but the boat continued its slow progress. Martin was now forming a human bridge between the boat and the pole, and Padraic was being stretched to the limit.

'Argh! This is it, Martin – I think we're going overboard!'

'Thanks for the support, P.'

A shout came from the front of the boat. 'Keep hold of him, Padraic! It's only water, don't be a chicken.'

'Where's the chicken?!?! Let me at him!' Padraic snapped, as his eyes darted around the boat, terrified.

'No, P!' Martin yelped. But it was too late – the distraction had caused Padraic to let go of Martin's feet.

Martin sprang to the pole, wrapping his legs around it. As the troop very slowly sailed further into the middle of Boyle Lake, he was left stranded on the pole, hanging on for dear life.

'All right boys, use your paws as paddles!' Gerry shouted.

The Scouts tried to use their hands to turn the boat around. There was quite a lot of confused splashing. There also seemed to be some crying, but that may just have been splashback.

'Buddy, this isn't going brilliantly,' I said.

'Hold on Martin, we're nearly there!' Gerry called.

Slowly, and beautifully, Martin's pole started tipping over, like a sad felled fir in the forest.

Splash!

The water was cold, but rather refreshing. The troop were impressed when Martin hit the surface and was somehow still bravely holding on to the boat pole.

'I can't hold it! I can't hold it any more!' he hollered.

'Don't worry, I've got it now,' Gerry said, as he wrestled the pole from the lake bed.

'I can't hold it! I can't hold it!'

'You don't need to hold it any more!' Gerry said, confused.

Finally, Martin stopped panicking. Slowly, his face became filled with calm and pure relief. He had stopped holding it.

'Is he . . . ?' asked Crunchie.

I nodded. 'Yep.'

'Well at least he's finally at one with nature.'

Martin smiled contentedly. He was a man reborn. But as he continued to tread water, he turned to find the entire troop staring down at his oddly happy face.

'I think Moone's got the right idea. Who's up for a swim?' asked Gerry. He pulled off his jumper and leapt into the lake.

'Ahh, the water's warm! *Really* warm. C'mon gang!'

A yelp went up from the troop as they all dived into the lake.

'Eh. I think I'll pass,' Padraic whispered, as he winked at his peeing pal.

YECTION 4

GOLDEN DAYS

HOMEWORK

The end of the school year can be a tough time. Lots of homework, exams, and the realization that you slept through every single geography class this year! Luckily, Martin's got his trusty imaginary friend to help him with his homework.

'Hey Moone! Stop writing that book! I need help with my homework and I've got to drive this bus back to London. The bobbies are after me!'

'Okey dokey, Mr Mannion, sir!'

Wow – Declan's homework! What an honour!

Declan Mannion is a legend in Boyle. He's been in sixth class forever – he's basically a grown man. So let's help Martin do Declan's homework. It shouldn't be too hard – his teacher, Mister Jackson, always gives him the easiest questions, just to try and get rid of him! And try not to mess it up so Martin can avoid one of Declan's 'reverse-wedgies' or 'Cambodian Burns' (a technique similar to the Chinese Burn, but on completion, it reveals Declan's name on his victim's forearm).

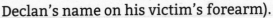

DECLAN WOZ ERE

ACTIVITY

DECLAN'S HOMEWORK

FROM MISTER JACKSON

1. Which teacher should you never make fun of?

    a) Mister Jackson.

    b) Mister Jackson.

    c) Mister Jackson.

    d) All of the above.

2. What should I not do with walls?

    a) Graffiti them.

    b) Smash them.

    c) Stick snots on them.

    d) All of the above.

3. If we had four class goldfish, and three of them disappeared, how many would be left?

    a) One lonely goldfish.

    b) I know you did it.

    c) If you return them unharmed, I won't get the police involved.

    d) Or was it the Bonner Brothers?

4. Why are you repeating sixth class yet again?

    a) Because you just don't listen.

    b) Because you spend more time at the greyhound racing track than you do in class.

    c) Because you want to torment me.

    d) All of the above.

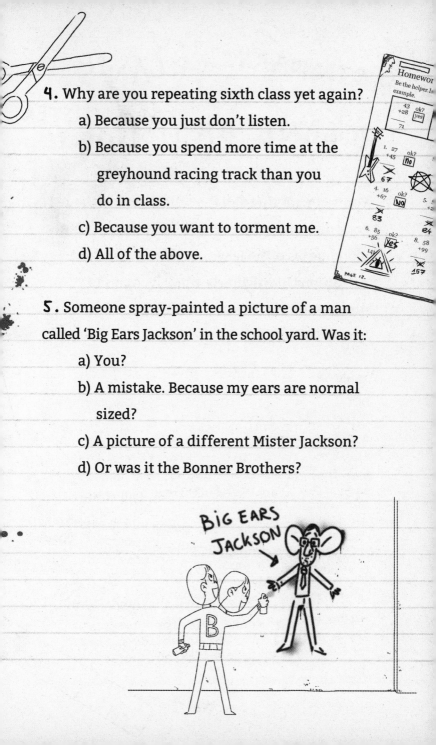

Homewor
Be the helper. Is
example.

43
+28   ok?
71   yes

1. 27   ok?
+45   no
67

4. 16   ok?
+67   no
83

6. 85   ok?
+56   yes
141

5.
+2
84

8. 58
+99
157

PAGE 12.

5. Someone spray-painted a picture of a man called 'Big Ears Jackson' in the school yard. Was it:

    a) You?

    b) A mistake. Because my ears are normal sized?

    c) A picture of a different Mister Jackson?

    d) Or was it the Bonner Brothers?

BiG EARS
JACKSON →

MOONE DICTIONARY

You can't get through the school year without a good dictionary by your side. But even the best dictionaries often leave out some important definitions, particularly when it comes to understanding IFs – which is why you need a Moone Dictionary!

AMADÁN — word number 79 for 'idiot'. This one's in Irish.

A BONNER BEATIN' — a rural type of sibling assault. It's a bit muckier than a standard beating, with more cursing, and usually ends with a double-dunk into a cowpat.

CHINESE BURN — a violent massage of the forearm that turns the skin red-hot. In ancient China this was done to warm pots of tea.

CIÚNAS — the Irish word for 'quiet'. It's usually shouted at children very loudly, which is confusing.

CORK — a county in Ireland where we send all the troublemakers. Like an Irish Texas. But everyone there thinks that Cork is bigger than Texas.

CRAIC — pronounced 'crack'. Another Irish word for 'fun'. Although no one seems to know for sure what it means, as a lot of conversations in Ireland start with the question 'What's the craic?'

GARDA — the Irish word for 'police'. Because they're like guards. Sorta.

GAS — a word Irish people use for 'fun'. It's said that the Eskimos have twenty-seven different words for snow. It's the same with the Irish and fun. And we're both freezing most of the time, so maybe that makes us smarter. Who knows?

GENIE MAC — Cork talk meaning 'flippin' heck!'. A Genie Mac is also a type of burger, like a Big Mac, but served in a lamp.

GRUAIGE — pronounced 'grew-a-gah'. The Irish word for 'hair'. In Ireland, many people have red hair. This is of course because the first-ever Irish woman married a fire extinguisher.

HAPPY AS LARRY — this expression refers to Larry Stapleton. He was well known as a happy person. Nothing else is known about him.

IFFY — the annual back-slapping procession for imaginary friends. Similar to the Oscars in almost no way at all.

NOLLAIG SHONA DHUIT — Irish for 'Merry Christmas to you'. The Irish word for 'Christmas' is 'Nollaig'. Which is why in Ireland, Father Christmas is called Noel. Dr Noel Christmas.

RADICAL! — word of exclamation popular with schoolboys in the 1980s. Other big hits that decade included 'Bodacious!', 'Extreme!', and 'Nud!' As in, 'That's totally nud!'

REALSIE — a non-imaginary. Someone you can poke.

SOUND — an Irish term for 'OK'. We used to say 'sshwwiggadingdonggg!' but shortened that sound to 'sound' as we're so busy nowadays.

ST BRENDAN — patron saint of bongo players. And lost cats.

SUMMERTIME MAD — a type of craziness that sets in when children have too much freedom. Symptoms include whistling, daydreaming, kite-making, raft-building, excessive laughter and too much general happiness.

WHISHT — the Irish equivalent of 'Shush', but a bit wetter, like most things Irish.

YOU'RE A POST — an Irish insult for someone who is as thick as a plank of wood or as lost as a piece of mail.

YOUSE — the plural of 'you', pronounced 'yooze'. Irish pronouns are organized like this: Us, them, you, yer man, yer wan, ye, youse, you lot, them lot, the lot of them, what's-his-name, what's-her-face, the fella over there, that shower of chancers behind the gate.

ACTIVITY
WHIF WHIST

 Martin isn't the only one who needs to do their homework. You can't create an imaginary friend without first doing some research. Check out these IFs and rate them on their skills and characteristics. It should help you figure out what you would and wouldn't like in your new IF. Mark each characteristic out of ten (or a million, if you've got loads of time), and then you can add them up to see who's the best.

Felicity Frump

Age ~~8~~ 39 .... ◯

Special skills PUMPKIN MAGIC ◯

Hobbies BARE-KNUCKLE FIGHTING ◯

Total score = ◯

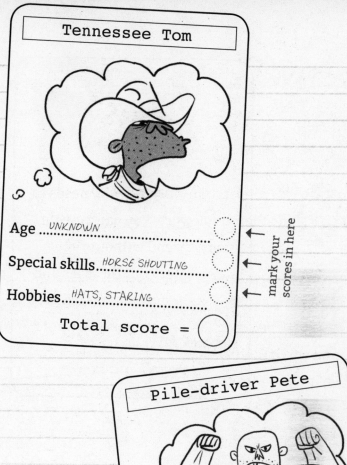

Tennessee Tom

Age ....UNKNOWN..........

Special skills ....HORSE SHOUTING....

Hobbies ....HATS, STARING....

Total score =

mark your scores in here

Pile-driver Pete

Age ..34..

Special skills ..PILE-DRIVING..

Hobbies ....SALSA DANCING....

Total score =

Loopy Lou

Age ..46......................................

Special skills..BALLOON ANIMALS....

Hobbies..EATING FRUITY LOOPS....

Total score = ⬡

Using these IF cards as a template, you could now make your own set of WHIF WHIST cards to play with by drawing your own pictures or cutting faces out of a magazine. Once you've made a load of cards, grab your friends, some snacks and your best poker face, and settle down for a game.

ACTIVITY

HOW TO PLAY WHIF WHIST

1. Deal all your cards out equally among the players.

2. Pick someone to choose a category from their top card.

3. Everyone else should look for the same category on their card, and whoever has the highest score wins the 'trick'.

4. The winner should do a victory dance and then collect all of the cards from that round, placing them at the bottom of their pile and choosing a new category for the next round.

5. If two or more cards have the same top value, these cards go in a pile in the middle and the same player chooses another category.

6. The winner of the round takes the cards they won plus the cards from the middle as well.

7. The person with all the cards at the end is the winner!

THE
AMAZING
ADVENTURES
OF
GERBIL GENT
~~IF MAN~~
AND
MOLE BOY
~~MOONE BOY~~!

Don't forget to colour us in!

. continued from page 71

121

122

IS HE FLYING?

WELL HE *IS* A PIGEON

COO COO COOLIO! THANKS LADS. SEE YA NOW

WHO WAS THAT PHANTOM PIGEON?!

IT *WAS* PADRAIC. IT WAS OBVIOUSLY PADRAIC. HE WASN'T EVEN WEARING A MASK.

NAH, HIS HAIR WAS DIFFERENT. HE HAD A KINDA CURL IN THE FRONT.

YEAH, IT COULD'VE BEEN ANYONE REALLY.

IT WAS PADRAIC!

BUT HE DID SPECIFICALLY SAY THAT HE WASN'T PADRAIC.

WOW. A REAL SUPERHERO IN BOYLE! WHO'D HAVE THOUGHT IT?

EAT THAT, GALWAY!

BUT THERE'S ALREADY A SUPERHERO IN BOYLE! ME! I GOT BITTEN BY A MOLE!

A MOLE? WHO CARES ABOUT MOLES?

A PIGEON — NOW THAT'S A SUPER ANIMAL!

PIGEONS? I'LL SHOW THEM. I'M THE SUPERHERO OF BOYLE! ME! ARGGHH!

WOW! ARE YOU ABOUT TO SMASH YOUR WAY OUT OF THAT BIN?

YOU BET! A BIN IS NO MATCH FOR MOLE BOY!

128

131

132

THE END

YECTION 5

DAYS OF WONDER

In Boyle the sun comes out three times every summer – on the 11 July, and the 4 and 5 of August. And boy are we ready for it! As soon as we spy the first rays of sunshine, Martin and I hop on our bike and peg it down to the lake as fast as we can, where Padraic, Trevor and all the gang are already splashing around. Then it's swimming and popsicles and lashings of sunburn until dusk. Once night sets in, Declan Mannion will usually set something on fire – a small shrub perhaps – and we'll all sit around and toast marshmallows (which everyone is forced to hand over to Declan because he says he owns the fire).

ACTIVITY

TREVOR'S MOTHER'S S'MORES

One night, Trevor showed us all how to make one of his mother's recipes for some weird magical thingies called s'mores. The name makes them sound like a skin disease, but they are in fact insanely delicious. See if you can make them too!

INGREDIENTS:

- Marshmallows
- Digestive biscuits
- A chocolate bar

DIRECTIONS:

1. Take one stick. Shove a marshmallow on to it and toast it over a fire until it's gooey.

2. Then lay it on your digestive biscuit.

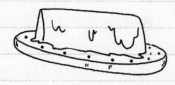

3. Then put some chocolate on top (about four squares should do it). The hot marshmallow will help it start to melt.

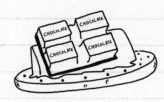

4. Then put another digestive on top to make a sandwich. Shove it in your gob and begin your journey to dessert heaven.

ACTIVITY

RATE THE MATE

Without school getting in the way, you've got a lot more time to think about your perfect IF. You might have some good ideas for them by now, but before you commit, don't forget to consider all the options. You don't have to choose a human-shaped IF like me. Here are a few other types of IFs for you to review, rate and name. You can use these cards to play WHIF WHIST too!

Age ....

Special skills ....

Hobbies ....

Total score = ( )

mark your scores in here like page 116

Age ....

Special skills ....

Hobbies ....

Total score = ( )

Age ....

Special skills...............................

Hobbies..................................

Total score = ◯

Age ....

Special skills...............................

Hobbies..................................

Total score = ◯

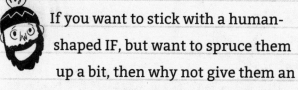 If you want to stick with a human-shaped IF, but want to spruce them up a bit, then why not give them an interesting appendage or accessory, like these!

A BEARD.
It's a classic for a reason.

IF WINGS.
Caution: Having a flying IF might give you a sore neck from looking up.

IF tail.

Available in all colours, hairy or slimy.

A bottomless handbag.

It worked for Mary Poppins.

IF TRUNK.

NOW YOU CAN ACTUALLY PAY YOUR IF IN PEANUTS!

WOODEN LEG.

They're not just for pirates, you know!

THE VERY ODD JOB

Martin thrust his head out of the back door and sucked in a noseful of autumn air.

'Ahh, the sweet scent of the Sixth Yection,' he sighed contentedly.

'Smells like soggy leaves and back-to-school sadness,' I mused.

'And old cheese,' Martin added, wrinkling his nose.

I nodded, picking it up too. 'Yep, I'm getting a mouldy cheddar whiff as well. And . . . hairspray, is it?'

'*Tons* of hairspray,' agreed Martin. 'And . . . What *is* that?' He sniffed again, perplexed. 'Kinda smells like a dead donkey!'

Martin then turned to see his sister, Sinead, standing right behind him. Which explained a lot.

'Oh hi, Sinead!' he said chirpily. 'Is that a new perfume from Pound Bargainz?'

'*Fragrance of Deceased Mule* perhaps?' I suggested.

Fragrance of
Deceased Mule

Martin tried to hide his grin, but his sister's eyes narrowed.

'Why are you wearing your goofus get-up?' she demanded.

'My what?'

'Your clod costume. Your sap suit.'

She gestured at his clothes, and Martin finally understood. 'Ah! You mean my handsome Scouts uniform! Well, you wouldn't know much about this, Sinead – since you got thrown out of the Girl Guides for trying to imprison your Patrol Leader, Missus O'Dwyer. But for us Scouts, it's Bob-a-Job week!'

Sinead grabbed him by the woggle. 'Firstly, Missus O'Dwyer was asking for it. Secondly,

I *chose* to leave to form a much better organization called The Flippin' Furious Females, which no one can join except for me! And thirdly – what the heck are you blathering on about?'

'Bob-a-Job week!' repeated Martin, wriggling out of her woggle-hold. 'The Scouts do it every year to raise money. We're all supposed to go out and do odd jobs around the neighbourhood, and folks will pay us a few "*bob*" for each "*job*". Get it?'

Sinead sighed. 'You really are a quality spanner.'

'Well I think that's great, Martin. Fair play to you!' called his mam from the kitchen table. She had all their bills spread out before her and was busy adding up their debts on a calculator. 'As my grandad used to say – *You're never too young to join the workforce – now get up that chimney!* Hahaha.'

She chuckled at this, but Martin and I just

145

looked at each other, confused. 'Your mam was a chimney sweep? *How old is she?!*' I asked in wonder.

'Well Martin,' said his dad, pacing around as he pored over a lottery scratch card. 'After twenty years of sign-writing, I can tell you this. There's nothing more satisfying than doing an honest day's work. And no amount of money will ever make you as happy as . . .' Liam stopped dead, scratching the card. 'Hold the phone, lads. I just got another ten thousand!'

'That's two ten thousands!' squealed Debra excitedly.

Liam looked ecstatic. 'One more ten thousand and I'll never have to look at another miserable sign ever again!'

He feverishly scratched the card.

But a moment later, his face fell and he gave a sad whimper.

'Five,' he announced glumly, and Debra sagged back in her seat.

Liam looked up and saw that Martin and the

girls were all looking at him.

'Eh. Like I was saying, jobs are great fun!' he continued. 'And an honest day's work is worth ten times more than any pay cheque!'

He got down on the floor and started picking up the little flecks that he'd scratched off the lottery ticket. 'Now help me gather up all these little scratchy bits, will ye? Maybe I can stick them back on to this useless lottery ticket and get my money back!'

That week, Martin managed to talk his way into doing a few back-breaking jobs. He swept up a neighbour's leaves on the gustiest hill in Boyle, he chopped up kindling for his grandad's fire, and he mowed the massive lawn and tennis court at his friend Trevor's house. But he was dismayed at how little money he earned.

'How much do I owe ya?' asked his grandad, when Martin had stacked a neat pile of twigs by the fireplace.

'Well it's a *suggested donation*, Grandad. So

there's no limit to how much you can give me!' Martin told him optimistically.

But unfortunately Grandad's 'suggestion' consisted of a few broken biscuits and a friendly thumbs-up.

Our most profitable job actually came from Martin's sister Trisha.

'I'll give ya ten pence if ya punch yourself in the gut,' she offered.

Martin considered this. 'Hmm. How about twenty pence if I punch myself in the ear?' he countered.

'Fifteen if you wedgie yourself.'

'Thirty if I stamp on my own foot and bite my tongue.'

'Twenty five if you stick chewing gum in your hair.'

'OK, here's the best combo deal I can offer

you, Trish,' said Martin flatly. 'For fifty pence, I'll punch myself in the ear, break an egg on my head, and run into that wall over there.'

'Done!' she agreed, and they shook hands happily.

'Fifty pence! What a sucker!' I laughed. 'Easy money!'

Trisha handed over the shiny coin and waited expectantly. Martin's smile faded, realizing that he now had to actually beat himself up.

'C'mon buddy!' I said brightly. 'Your customer's waiting!'

He gulped deeply, and then slugged* himself in his lugs**.

---

*SLUGGED — punched. This gets its name because long ago slugs used to be ferocious fighters. But one day, they discovered love. And now they just slither around, French-kissing everything they touch.

**LUGS — another word for 'ears'. Short for 'luggage handles', because if you ever checked your head in at an airport, this is how they'd pick you up.

MOONE DICTIONARY

By Friday, Martin's earnings were still pretty slim, and he was starting to get desperate. 'What am I gonna do, P-bear?' he asked Padraic, as they paced around the school yard. 'I can't keep punching myself for money!'

'And I can't keep eating stones for cash!' agreed Padraic glumly. 'My intestines weigh a ton, and I haven't had a poo in four days!'

'Right,' said Martin, nodding in sympathy as he remembered his own toilet troubles from their recent camping trip. 'This can't go on,' he agreed. 'We need a proper job. And we need it now!'

'A job, you say?' came a familiar voice skulking up behind us.

We turned to see Martin's charismatic classmate Declan Mannion. He wore a leather trench-coat over his school uniform, and he was gnawing on a toothpick. (It was actually a little stick for cocktail sausages – he'd crashed a three-year-old's birthday party earlier that day and stolen a plate of appetisers.)

'Then it's your lucky day,' said Declan, with a grin. 'I just so happen to be looking for a couple of fellas to do a few . . . "odd jobs" for me.'

Martin's eyes lit up. 'Then look no further, Mister Mannion, sir! We're your odd-jobbers!'

'How much does it pay?' asked Padraic eagerly. 'I mean, how much do you . . . suggest you donate?'

Declan chewed on his cocktail-sausage stick, considering this.

'Before we negotiate,' interjected Martin, 'I should point out that we are desperate!'

'Good thinking, buddy,' I said. 'Always good to make that clear.'

'I'll give ye a tenner each,' offered Declan.

'A tenner?!' I spluttered. 'That's worth twenty ear thumps!'

'Woohoo!' cried Martin, and high-fived Padraic. Then he said to Declan grandly, 'We accept your offer, Mister Mannion.'

'Good stuff. Meet me outside the old junkyard at midnight,' said the mysterious Mannion. He turned to go, but then glanced back. 'Oh – and bring some rashers.'

He swaggered away, leaving the boys looking confused.

'Rashers in a junkyard at midnight?' asked Martin. 'What kind of odd job *is* this?'

'Oh I wouldn't worry about it, buddy,' I reassured him. 'It's probably just some kinda late-night . . . bacon-eating . . . mechanic work?'

Padraic looked very uneasy. 'I've got a bad feeling about this, Martin.' There was a strange rumble in his stomach, and then his face brightened. 'No, wait – that was just the stones shifting. Now I've got a better feeling about it!'

The town clock struck midnight as Martin and Padraic arrived at the junkyard. On the way over, they'd raided a dumpster outside Padraic's auntie's butcher shop for old rashers that were past their sell-by date, and now their pockets were bulging with bacon. Declan was lurking in the shadows around the back of the junkyard, peering through the wire fence at the collection of crushed cars, rusted trucks, and assorted piles of metal that were strewn about the place.

'Hiya, Declan!' called Martin, as they approached.

'Shhhh!' he hissed. 'Keep it down, Moone.'

Martin paused. 'Why?' he whispered, blankly. 'Are we not . . . supposed to be here?'

'Eh . . . No, no – nothing like that. It's just that I've . . . got a bit of a sore ear,' he explained.

'Gotcha,' whispered Martin. After slugging his lugs earlier, he was all too familiar with sore ears.

'So what are these odd jobs you need doing?' asked Padraic, eager to get started.

'Oh I just need you to do a few chores for me in there,' Declan told them, gesturing at the junkyard. 'A bit of trimming, a bit of tidying, that sort of thing.'

'No problemo!' replied Padraic chirpily.

But Martin looked less sure as he glanced

through the wire. 'Whose junkyard is this?' he asked.

'It's eh . . . It's mine,' said Declan simply. 'I own it.'

'You own your own junkyard?!'

'He's got his finger in every pie, that fella,' whispered Padraic in awe.

Martin couldn't help but feel a bit jealous. It was one of his lifelong dreams to own a junkyard, but now Declan had beaten him to it! I guess he'd just have to focus on the next dreams on his list – owning a trained swan, and teaching it how to rescue him from quicksand.

'But I lost the keys to the gate,' Declan went on, 'and I'm locked out.'

I snorted with laughter. 'Ha! Well that's embarrassing. Mister "I own my own junkyard" is locked out of his own junkyard! The big idiot.'

'So your first chore is to trim a nice big hole in that fence.' He gave them each a pair of wire cutters. 'Oh and pop these on first, will ye?'

He handed them each a black woolly hat. At least, they *thought* they were hats, until they noticed the eye-holes in them.

'Balaclavas?' asked Martin, alarmed.

'They're just to keep your faces warm,' explained Declan.

'Makes sense. No one likes a cold face while cutting a hole in a fence!' noted Padraic.

'But don't . . . *thieves* usually wear these?' asked Martin uneasily.

'Ah no, all sorts of people wear them!' Declan informed him. 'My dad wears one to the office sometimes. Or even when we're a bit chilly in the house. They're just handy face-warmers.'

'My face *does* feel a lot snugger now,' confirmed Padraic, who was already wearing his balaclava.

Martin gave a shrug and pulled on the woolly face mask.

The boys got to work with the wire cutters, and soon they had carved out an impressive hole.

'Done!' they cried. 'What's our next chore, boss?'

Declan poked his head through the gap and peered around.

'Well, the whole yard needs a good clean-up. So grab all the copper wire you can find, and haul it out here, while I keep a look-out.'

'Got it,' said Martin. 'Wait – a look-out for what?'

'Oh. Eh. Friends . . . ?' said Declan, with a shrug. 'Passers-by? I love to keep a look-out for folks, so I can wave to them. And just . . . say hello.'

'Aww,' said Martin, touched.

'Now get a move on!' Declan snapped.

The boys saluted and hopped through the hole.

'People give Declan such a bad rap, but he must be the friendliest fella in Boyle,' noted Padraic happily, as they strolled through the junkyard in their balaclavas.

'Totally!' agreed Martin. 'I don't know why people say he can't be trusted. He's clearly misunderstood. People just don't get him.'

'But we totally get him! Now, let's find his copper wire and clean it the flip out of this place!'

The boys high-fived and ran off in opposite directions to search the heaps of scrap.

A few minutes later, Martin and I were digging

through a pile of old engines.

'Any luck?' called Martin.

'Not yet,' I said. 'You?'

'Nope.'

I paused my search. 'Hey, one quick question, Martin – what exactly *is* copper wire?'

'Haven't a clue,' he admitted. 'I was hoping *you'd* know.'

'Is it "copper" like a "policeman"? Do the police carry around rolls of wire?'

Martin shrugged blankly. 'Maybe he said *chopper* wire,' he suggested.

'What's chopper wire?'

'Like, wire for helicopters?'

'I don't think that's a thing.'

'OK. Well let's just keep our eyes peeled for police wire and helicopter wire – and then we can't go wrong.'

'Good thinking!'

Just then, we heard a terrified screech across the junkyard and we looked up to see Padraic galloping towards us, with what looked like a coil of wire slung over his shoulder.

'MARTIN!!!' he shrieked, leaping like a chubby gazelle* over rusted bicycles and busted televisions.

A ferocious one-eyed dog was in hot pursuit, yapping and snarling at his heels.

'Aw balls,' I gulped, as they tore across the yard towards us.

'Why are you running *towards me*?!!' Martin shouted at Padraic. 'Run away from me! Run the other way!'

'Which way?!!' panted Padraic, as he bore down on us.

'Any other way!'

But it was too late.

A moment later, we were all running together, with the dog scrambling after us. We raced around an old cement truck several

---

*GAZELLE — a kind of deer. Like Martin and Padraic, they are the fastest run-away-ers in the animal kingdom.

MOONE DICTIONARY

times before we heard a voice.

'Quick – in here!'

It was Padraic's imaginary friend, Crunchie Haystacks! He was sitting in the front of the truck and we dived in after him. The dog tried to follow, his jaws aimed at Padraic's round rump, but we slammed the door just in time, and it got a mouthful of metal instead.

'Phew!' we gasped, as the boys pulled off their sweaty balaclavas.

'Well that was a close one!' chuckled Crunchie.

'What are you doing here?' I asked.

'What's *who* doing here?' asked Martin, cluelessly – as he couldn't actually see or hear the hairy wrestler beside us.

'Crunchie!' explained Padraic. 'I imagined him in the nick of time! He saved us!'

'Oh, it's just part of the job,' said Crunchie

bashfully. 'That's what IFs are for – saving our Realsies from DANGER!!' he cried, pulling a wrestling pose.

But we were still most definitely in danger. The dog was circling around us, gnawing at the tyres hungrily.

'Moone!' came a voice in the distance.

We looked across the junkyard to see Declan Mannion peering through the hole in the fence.

'Moone!' he hissed. 'Use the bacon!'

'The what?'

'The bacon!'

Declan mimed chomping on a rasher.

'Is he saying that you should . . . eat the bacon?' I asked.

'Of course!' declared Martin. 'If we eat the bacon, we'll have enough strength to fight the dog!'

Padraic looked unsure. 'I don't think any amount of bacon is going to make me brave enough for that.'

'Come on, P. It's our only chance. Eat up!'

The boys pulled out their slices of dodgy bacon and tried to chew them up. But this proved to be more difficult than expected. Padraic tried to swallow a rasher whole, but it caught in his gullet and he coughed it up, sending it flying out the window. The dog pounced on the revolting rasher, devouring it – and at the same moment, Declan Mannion pulled open the door and hopped inside.

'Nice work, Padraic. Well done for distracting him!'

'No problemo, Mister Mannion!' coughed a confused Padraic, as he hocked up another piece of bacon.

'Little Stabteeth is a bit peckish,' explained Declan. 'I forgot to give him his dinner.'

He flung the remaining rashers out the window, and Stabteeth started wolfing them down. Declan then pulled out a bunch of wires from underneath the steering wheel, as if he was hot-wiring the truck.

'Don't you have a key?' asked Martin.

'Eh . . . I lost those ones as well,' said Declan sheepishly.

'Somebody get this guy a key ring!' I chuckled, shaking my head.

Suddenly the engine roared into life. Declan put his foot down and the truck leapt forward.

'Hang on, lads!' he called with a grin.

There wasn't much to hang on to, so the boys hung on to each other. We barrelled towards the main gate and then smashed right out of the junkyard.

'Woohoo!' cried Padraic.

'Well that solves the locked gate problem!' said Martin. 'Though maybe you should think about leaving a spare key under a pot plant or something next time,' he suggested.

'Great idea, Moone. I never thought of that!'

Martin and I chuckled quietly at his absent-mindedness.

'I guess some folks are just too stupid to see

the most obvious things,' I said, as we tore off
into the night.

Declan dropped us at Martin's house and
Padraic handed him the coil of copper wire.

'Well done, my little bob-a-jobbers,' said Declan. 'We trimmed, we tidied, we fed the dog, and fixed the truck. A good night's work all round.'

'Happy to help, Mister Mannion sir!' replied the pair, basking in a job well done.

Declan cocked his head. In the distance, we could hear sirens.

'Must be a fire somewhere,' noted Padraic.

'Nah, it's probably just an ice-cream truck,' said Declan. 'Maybe I'll get myself a nice breakfast choc-ice. Adios, compadres!'

He gave a wink, flicked his greasy hair out of his eyes, and sped away in the cement truck.

Dawn was just beginning to break as Martin and Padraic bid farewell.

'Til next time, Baloo.'

'See ya, Dumbo.'

They did their secret Scout handshake and then Padraic strolled off towards his home.

As we made our way up the driveway, Martin

gave a little shudder. 'It's a bit chilly this morning, isn't it?'

'Want to put on your face warmer?' I suggested.

Martin pulled on his balaclava and felt a lot cosier as we made our way around the back of the house towards his bedroom window. 'You know, I think Dad's right. There's nothing more satisfying than doing an honest day's work.'

I nodded, and then paused. 'Wait a second. Wasn't Declan supposed to *pay* you?'

Martin stopped. 'Aw balls.'

'Don't worry, buddy, it was probably just an oversight.'

He shook his head with annoyance. 'How could someone so forgetful end up owning their own junkyard?'

I shrugged. 'Just another Mannion mystery,' I said in wonder.

Martin climbed in through his bedroom window. But as he poked his little balaclava'd head through the curtains, his sister Sinead jumped up and gave a scream.

'Argh! A burglar!'

'No, it's me—' he started.

But she was already whacking him ferociously with a tennis racquet.

'OW! My tennis ankle!' he shrieked.

More lights went on, more of his family scrambled out of bed, and soon the whole countryside could hear the dawn chorus of yelling Moones.

YECTION G

WONDER WHAT HAPPENED TO THE NEW SCHOOL YEAR?

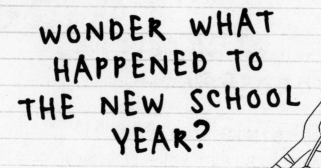

Summer's over already?! Aw balls. Back-to-school time is the worst. The only fun thing about it is buying new school supplies. Help fill Martin's pencil case by finding everything he needs in this wordsearch.

PENCIL   CATAPULT   DIARY

RULER   PEN   PAPER

PROTRACTOR   NOTEBOOK   AEROPLANE

COMPASS   CALCULATOR

ERASER   PAPERCLIP

R	T	W	S	N	U	K	A	D	R	R	C	W	O
P	A	P	E	R	A	E	R	O	P	L	A	N	E
A	P	I	B	L	T	H	M	Q	I	O	T	S	R
P	N	D	W	H	D	R	V	C	Y	P	A	E	E
E	A	O	F	J	L	D	N	L	M	F	P	S	T
R	B	N	N	N	T	E	P	D	N	F	U	M	D
C	P	C	O	M	P	A	S	S	I	H	L	I	N
L	Z	A	Q	U	E	H	R	P	U	A	T	O	L
I	R	L	P	V	N	O	T	E	B	O	O	K	H
P	I	C	O	O	H	L	F	H	W	Y	I	A	E
S	B	U	A	F	L	N	H	D	S	E	W	S	D
H	I	L	E	S	K	R	N	B	I	R	U	S	H
F	G	A	O	N	L	A	U	I	G	A	J	E	W
M	C	T	W	H	I	E	O	L	B	S	R	G	O
Z	L	O	T	L	S	I	N	I	E	E	H	Y	T
U	P	R	O	T	R	A	C	T	O	R	L	A	E

Answers on page 195

169

ACTIVITY

THE HAND STAND

Have you ever had your hand up in a lesson for so long that your arm has gone to sleep? Look no further than the hand stand, to take all the pressure away from trying to answer a question.

1. Draw around your hand on a piece of card.

2. Cut it out.

3. Sellotape lots of pencils together into a long stick.

4. Tape the card hand on to the stick and hold it in the air when you need it.

ACTIVITY

MAZE GAME

In *Moone Boy: The Fish Detective*, Martin came up with a genius idea to shorten his route to school – he made a hole in his garden wall. But now his dad's closed it up and Martin has to go the regular way. Can you help him find his way to school?

Answer on page 196

START

FINISH

ACTIVITY

BONNER BROTHERS' CRAFT CORNER

'Out of the way, Moone! We're doing this bit. We love scaring folks, so Halloween is our favourite time of year. It's the one day we're actually allowed to torment people – and we don't even need to use our torture table!'

'In fact, Halloween is so mixed up that some folks will even reward you for scaring them!

174

They give you sweets! And chocolate! And sometimes fruit. Which is really annoying. Those people deserve to be double scared!

So let's get to it! We've made a scary Halloween mask based on what we think Trevor's imaginary friend, Loopy Lou, looks like – or what we think he should look like. If we had an imaginary friend, he'd be so terrifying that we'd scream ourselves to sleep every night! But if you don't think this one's scary enough, we dare you to try something different. Make a vampire, a werewolf, a banshee, a zombie, or whatever you think our imaginary friend would look like. You might find some more inspiration in our Spooky Crossword on page 178.

1. Get some coloured card and cut it into the shape of the creature you want your mask to be – or use the picture of Loopy Lou on the next page as a basis to draw your own.

2. Cut out holes for your eyes and mouth,

175

making sure they match up to your face
(unless wonky eyes will help your scariness!).

3. Now it's time to spookify your mask. Use
paints, pencils, pens and other bits and
bobs you can find to make it as
petrifying as possible!

4. Make one small hole halfway down the
left and the right side of the mask. Cut a
piece of string to go around your head, pass
the ends through the holes in your mask, and
tie a knot to stop the string slipping out.

5. Get scaring!

6. Get sweets!

7. If you get fruit, scare even harder! Or just
ring their doorbell a few times and run
like mad!

ACTIVITY

SPOOKY CROSSWORD

ACROSS

3. Likes the taste of blood (7)
6. A big orange lantern (7)
10. What you chant at Halloween (5-2-5)
12. Lives in a haunted house (5)
13. An undead monster (6)

DOWN

1. The most famous vampire (7)
2. The sound that you make when you're frightened (6)
4. The bones of your body (8)
5. A witch's mode of transport (10)
7. He created a monster (12)
8. A person who changes at the full moon (8)
9. Sleeps upside down (3)
11. A spider's house (6)

178

Answers on page 197

179

YECTION 7
WHY WON'T IT END?

Christmas is coming! It's time to go shopping for presents. I like to Spot the Difference in the window of Cross Country Meats. See if you can find ten things missing in the right-hand picture.

ACTIVITY

SPOT
THE DIFFERENCE

ACTIVITY

FIDELMA'S CRAFT CORNER

'In *Moone Boy: The Fish Detective*, I made an Advent calendar, and behind each door there was a different heart-throb, much to Martin's annoyance. Make your own Advent calendar and populate it with some festive imaginary friends.'

1. Cut two identical Christmas trees out of thin card (big enough for 24 windows).

2. Draw 24 boxes on to one of your trees. Cut out images of popstars, superheroes, politicians or the IFs you've picked up along the way and stick them in each box.

182

3. On your second tree, draw 24 matching boxes and write the numbers 1–24 on them in your sparkliest pen.

4. VERY CAREFULLY cut around three sides of each box to make your doors.

5. Place one tree over the other and stick down around the edges. Make a star out of foil and stick it on the top.

6. Put your Advent calendar in pride of place, and take it in turns to see who is behind each door!

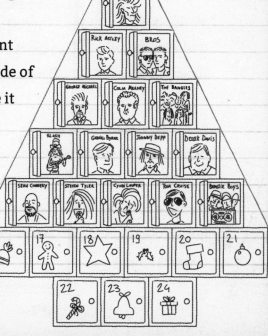

ACTIVITY BRIDGET CROSS'S CHRISTMAS COOKIES

Sé an rud is tábhachtaí sa ghnó bia, ná glantanas.

Oops! Sorry. Bridget Cross only speaks Irish. She's Padraic's aunt and gave Martin a job in her shop, Cross Country Meats, once. I think she is saying something about being unclean in the food business. So make sure you wash your hands before you make a start on these delicious gingerbread cookies.

INGREDIENTS:

- 350g plain flour, plus extra for dusting
- 1 teaspoon bicarbonate of soda
- 2 teaspoons ground ginger
- 1 teaspoon mixed spice
- 125g butter, chilled and cut into small pieces
- 175g light soft brown sugar
- 2 tablespoons golden syrup
- 1 egg (beaten)
- A cookie cutter in a Christmas shape (star/tree/bell)

DIRECTIONS:

1. Preheat the oven to 190° C/Gas Mark 5 and line two baking trays with baking paper.

2. Sift the flour into a bowl along with the bicarbonate of soda, ground ginger and mixed spice. Then rub in the butter until it looks like crumbs. Now add the sugar, golden syrup and egg, and stir it all together into a sticky dough. If it's too sticky, add a bit more flour to the mix.

3. Roll out the dough on a well-floured surface with a rolling pin until it is about 0.5 cm thick. Cut out your gingerbread shapes and, using a spatula, slide them on to the baking trays.

4. Bake for about 15 minutes until golden brown. When they are cool, decorate them with whatever you like – icing pens, hundreds and thousands, or chocolate sprinkles.

ACTIVITY CHRISTMAS DECORATIONS

While you're waiting for those cookies to cool, let's get the rest of the place ready. Pile the presents around the Christmas Tree and decorate it without electrocuting yourself like this:

ACTIVITY

UNWRAPPING YOUR IF

It's Christmas Day! The time has finally come to reap the rewards of everything you've learned in this marvellous manual. Unwrap your imaginary present and draw a picture of your new IF! Don't forget to include the things you've collected along the way – their nifty hat and outfit – and to write in their catchphrase.

189

And now it's time to party. Kick back, relax and colour us all in. Happy Christmas!

GOODBYE FROM ME

 Well I don't know about you, but I am pooped! I need a good lie-down after all that, and a cool glass of rumble juice. It's not easy making an imaginary friend. That's why I've never felt the urge to get one myself. They're nothing but trouble! Apart from yours truly, of course. But before we say farewell, let's do a quick survey.

Did you actually bother to create your own IF?

A. I sure did!

B. Nope, I've mostly been picking my nose.

C. Yes, but I've now lost him.

D. Oh, was I supposed to make an IF?

If you answered A, then well done, and you are welcome, my friend! I hope your new IF will keep you entertained until we meet again!

If you answered anything else, then you clearly didn't follow my instructions and you need to start this book again!

And while you do that, Martin and I are going to have a nice nap behind this wall.

Catch ya later, Moonies!

Caution

PUZZLE ANSWERS

HATS AHOY! PAGES 46-47

CATCHY
WORDSEARCH
PAGES 84-85

A	T	Y	S	A	J	K	F	M	L	A	R	H	S
G	Y	O	U	R	E	A	P	O	S	T	N	F	L
M	P	F	B	F	L	W	T	H	O	H	B	G	A
L	C	D	I	R	N	B	G	A	U	I	W	C	P
T	A	H	S	D	S	A	J	E	N	F	H	H	M
I	I	L	W	Y	D	L	Q	S	D	W	A	E	Y
H	I	X	O	R	R	L	Y	G	A	S	T	Y	B
F	J	T	P	K	J	S	E	A	G	T	S	N	E
W	H	I	S	H	T	Z	D	S	H	L	T	E	L
S	A	W	J	O	L	S	S	F	T	W	H	Y	L
W	P	O	A	S	N	I	L	E	W	I	E	J	Y
M	P	Q	H	T	S	M	U	L	R	D	C	L	Q
R	Y	R	G	N	R	H	C	L	Y	G	R	K	R
K	A	L	E	I	O	P	Y	A	U	J	A	T	S
P	S	D	N	Q	W	H	O	O	P	S	I	E	M
I	L	P	I	R	H	Y	E	G	K	B	C	W	L
W	A	F	E	C	U	Q	J	D	Z	P	I	F	S
K	R	S	M	L	A	V	E	L	I	J	P	O	D
Z	R	M	A	D	E	L	C	F	S	D	L	H	F
C	Y	N	C	G	K	A	M	A	D	A	N	K	A
X	I	Y	K	J	D	G	H	D	G	K	D	T	J

SCHOOL HEAD-SCRATCHER WORDSEARCH
PAGES 168-169

R	T	W	S	N	U	K	A	D	R	R	C	W	O
P	A	P	E	R	A	E	R	O	P	L	A	N	E
A	P	I	B	L	T	H	M	Q	I	O	T	S	R
P	N	D	W	H	D	R	V	C	Y	P	A	E	E
E	A	O	F	J	L	D	N	L	M	F	P	S	T
R	B	N	N	N	T	E	P	D	N	F	U	M	D
C	P	C	O	M	P	A	S	S	I	H	L	I	N
L	Z	A	Q	U	E	H	R	P	U	A	T	O	L
I	R	L	P	V	N	O	T	E	B	O	O	K	H
P	I	C	O	O	H	L	F	H	W	Y	I	A	E
S	B	U	A	F	L	N	H	D	S	E	W	S	D
H	I	L	E	S	K	R	N	B	I	R	U	S	H
F	G	A	O	N	L	A	U	I	G	A	J	E	W
M	C	T	W	H	I	E	O	L	B	S	R	G	O
Z	L	O	T	L	S	I	N	I	E	E	H	Y	T
U	P	R	O	T	R	A	C	T	O	R	L	A	E

195

SPOOKY CROSSWORD PAGES 178-179

	D				S								
	R				C								
V	A	M	P	I	R	E							
	C				E							B	
	U			S				F			R		
	L	P	U	M	P	K	I	N		R			
	A			E				R		O			
		W		L		B		A		O			
		E		E		A		N		M			
T	R	I	C	K	O	R	T	R	E	A	T		
		R		O		N		E		S			
		E	C	N				N		T			
		W	O			G	H	O	S	T			
		O	B					T		I			
		L	W		Z	O	M	B	I	E			
		F	E					N		K			
			B										

Across / Down answers:

1 DRACULA
2 SCREAM
3 VAMPIRE
4 SKELETON
5 BROOMSTICK
6 PUMPKIN
7 FRANKENSTEIN
8 WEREWOLF
9 BAT
10 TRICK OR TREAT
11 COBWEB
12 GHOST
13 ZOMBIE

197

HAVE YOU READ

Chris O'Dowd & Nick V. Murphy

MOONE BOY
THE FISH DETECTIVE

'RAUCOUSLY FUNNY' IRISH TIMES

UNDERCOVER OVERCOOKED

'HARD TO PUT DOWN'
THE BOOKBAG

'WE LOVE THIS
TIMELY STORY'
ANGELS AND URCHINS

'TOTALLY NUTTY, AND
VERY, VERY FUNNY'
LOVEREADING4KIDS

'RAUCOUSLY FUNNY'
IRISH TIMES

'UNIQUE AND
HILARIOUS'
SIDNEY, AGE 11

'I HOPE THIS IS
NOT THE LAST I
HAVE HEARD OF
MARTIN MOONE
AND SEAN MURPHY'
CAMERON, AGE 10

REVIEWS

HAVE YOU READ

Chris O'Dowd & Nick V. Murphy

MOONE BOY

THE BLUNDER YEARS

WINNER:
BORD GÁIS
IRISH
CHILDREN'S
BOOK AWARD

'HILARIOUS AND BRILLIANT'
FRANK COTTRELL BOYCE

'LAUGH-OUT-LOUD'
PRIMARY TIMES IRELAND

'A REAL HOOT, AND PERFECT FOR FANS OF DAVID WALLIAMS AND DIARY OF A WIMPY KID'
WRD MAGAZINE

'HIGHLY ORIGINAL, QUIRKY, FUNNY, HUGELY ENJOYABLE!'
BOOKS MONTHLY

'WILDLY ENTERTAINING . . . IF YOU MISS OUT ON STRAIGHT-UP CRAIC LIKE THIS, YOU ARE A GOMBEEN OF THE HIGHEST ORDER'
THE NEW YORK TIMES

'FULL OF GENTLE HUMOUR' WE LOVE THIS BOOK

'A TOTAL BALL! A LAUGH EVERY PAGE!'
EDWARD, AGE 10

'A BRILLIANTLY FUNNY READ FULL OF CRAZY CHARACTERS, HILARIOUS DEFINITIONS AND COOL CARTOONS. I LOVED IT!' SAM, AGE 11

ABOUT CHRIS O'DOWD

Chris O'Dowd is an award-winning actor and writer from the barmy town of Boyle in Ireland. Chris did some good acting in *Bridesmaids*, *The IT Crowd*, *Gulliver's Travels* and *Of Mice and Men*. We won't mention the films where he did bad acting. He has a dog called Potato and a cat who shouts at him for no reason. He studied at University College Dublin and the London Academy of Music and Dramatic Art. He graduated from neither. Chris created *Moone Boy* to get revenge on his sisters for putting make-up on him as a child. He co-wrote the Sky TV series and the *Moone Boy* books with his good friend Nick Murphy, who is a lot older than Chris.

ABOUT NICK V. MURPHY

Nick V. Murphy is a writer from Kilkenny, Ireland. (The V. in his name stands for Very.) He went to Trinity College Dublin to study English and History, but spent most of his time doing theatre and running away from girls. This was where he bumped into Chris O'Dowd, who was out looking for pizza. After college, Nick focused on writing, which was the laziest career he could think of, as it could even be done while wearing pyjamas. He wrote a few things for TV, then a movie called *Hideaways*, before co-writing a short film with Chris called *Capturing Santa*. The pyjama-wearing pair developed this into the comedy series *Moone Boy*, which recently won an International Emmy for Best Comedy.